This Little Tiger book belongs to:

_____

_____

_____

For Beatrice
~ A M
For my sister-in-law Jan
~ A E

LITTLE TIGER PRESS LTD,
an imprint of the Little Tiger Group
1 Coda Studios, 189 Munster Road, London SW6 6AW
Imported into the EEA by Penguin Random House Ireland,
Morrison Chambers, 32 Nassau Street, Dublin D02 YH68
www.littletiger.co.uk

First published in Great Britain 2014
This edition published 2015

A CIP catalogue record for this book is
available from the British Library

All rights reserved • ISBN 978-1-84895-748-0

Printed in China • LTP/1800/4723/0322

6 8 10 9 7 5

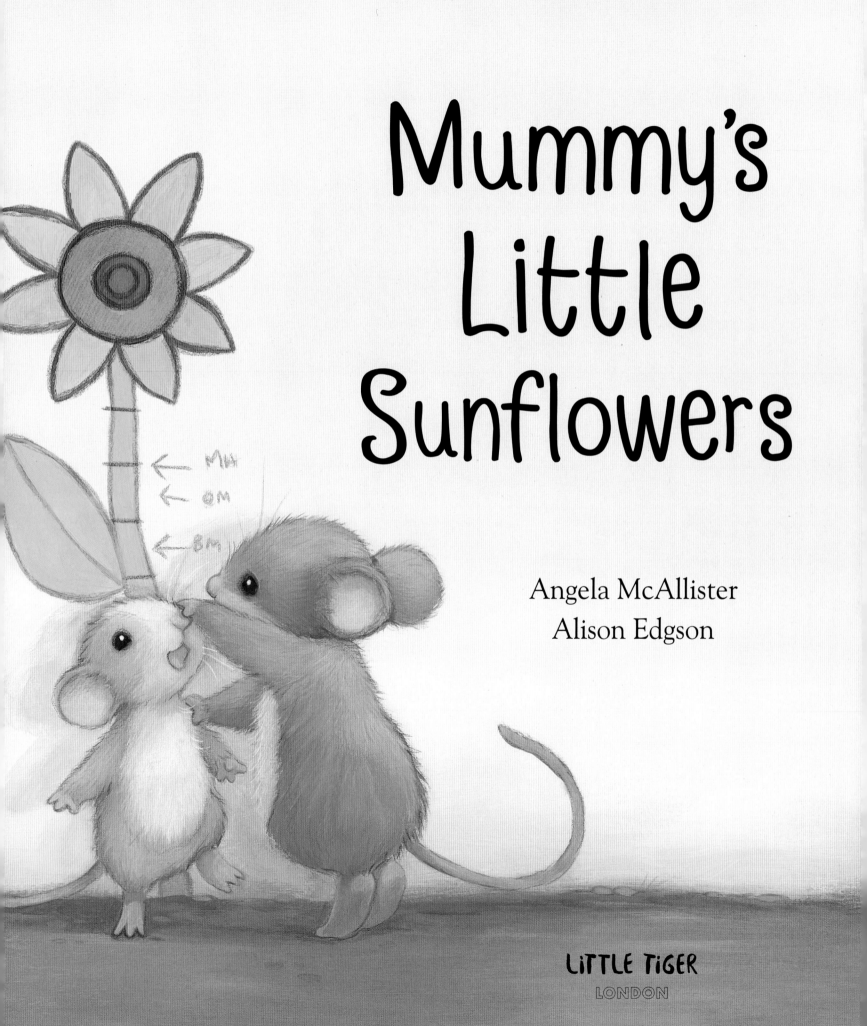

Mummy's Little Sunflowers

Angela McAllister

Alison Edgson

LITTLE TIGER
LONDON

Tiny Tots Nursery

"I'm a sunflower!" cried Scurry, racing out of nursery. "And look, Scamp, I've got a seed, so we can grow a sunflower just for Mummy!"

"Funflower!" giggled his little brother, skipping off.

"Slow down, Scamp," sighed Mummy. "You're always in such a hurry!"

The next morning, Scurry jumped out
of bed and raced to get his seed.
But it had disappeared!
A trail of crumbs led . . .

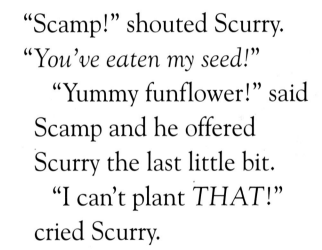

down the stairs . . .
and into the garden . . .

"Scamp!" shouted Scurry.
"You've eaten my seed!"
"Yummy funflower!" said
Scamp and he offered
Scurry the last little bit.
"I can't plant *THAT*!"
cried Scurry.

Blackbird flapped down.
   "Shhh! You're frightening the worms!"
he grumbled.
   "Scamp ate my sunflower seed!"
said Scurry.
   Scamp's whiskers drooped.
"I'm sorry," he squeaked.

"Well, no need to fuss,"
tutted Blackbird. "You'll
find plenty more sunflowers along
the lane."

"Ooh! Thank you," cried
Scurry happily. "Come
on, Scamp."

And off they ran.

Scamp raced ahead.

"I found a funflower!"
he cheered.

But as he rushed to
show Scurry . . .

Scamp tripped and fell . . .

SPLAT!

into a puddle!

"Funflower?" asked Scamp, pointing at his crumpled flower.

"No," said Scurry gently as he dried Scamp's whiskers, "that's a dandelion. Come on, we'll look together."

Holding paws, they skipped along the lane.
Scamp spotted lots of bright yellow flowers.
"There! There!" he squeaked excitedly.
But each time Scurry shook his head.
"Those are too tiny," he sighed.
"Sunflowers are BIG, Scamp . . . as BIG as . . ."

". . . THOSE!" gasped Scurry.
"How will we *ever* get up
there?"

Suddenly they heard a "MOO!"
  "Look! It's a cow! She can help us!"
cried Scamp. "Cooey, Cow! Cooey!"
  "Oh no!" squeaked Scurry.
"We'll get SQUASHED!"

"Hello," said Cow gently.
"Are you lost?"

"We want to see the sunflowers,"
said Scurry, shyly, "but we're
too small."

"I'm not!" said Cow. "I'll give
you a lift!"

Scamp and Scurry scrambled
onto Cow's curly head. Up, up, up
they went until they saw . . .

. . . hundreds of huge yellow sunflowers
waving in the breeze!

Scurry and Scamp jumped into the biggest
flower and munched delicious seeds
in the warm summer sun.
"Yummy, yummy!" Scamp smiled happily.

When their tummies were full, they collected
some seeds and Cow carried them down.
"Thank you!" they cried.

When they got home Scurry and Scamp
started planting. Then they poked and patted
and stamped and watered – it was messy work!

At teatime Scamp couldn't sit still.

"Grow, sunny funflowers, grow!" he sang,
bouncing on his chair.

He gobbled down his dinner and hurried
back outside without even licking his whiskers.

Suddenly Mummy and Scurry heard a cry . . .

They found Scamp in the
flowerbed, sobbing big fat tears.
"No funflowers for Mummy!"
he wailed.

For Mummy

"Oh dear, you're always in *such* a hurry, Scamp!" said Mummy, giving him a hug. "Flowers need lots of time to grow," Scurry explained, "and lots of sun and rain."

Then Scurry had an idea. "Come with me, Scamp."

That evening Mummy heard lots of giggling upstairs. And at bedtime she had a beautiful surprise . . .

"I'm a SUNFLOWER!" cried Scamp, grinning proudly.
"Hurray!" cheered Scurry.
"What a clever pair," said Mummy in amazement.
"I didn't need to wait for sun and rain. I have two
beautiful little sunflowers all of my very own!"